Kenneth Grahame's
THE WIND IN THE WILLOWS

The Battle at Toad Hall

Adapted by Janet Palazzo-Craig
Illustrated by Mary Alice Baer

TROLL ASSOCIATES

Library of Congress Cataloging in Publication Data

Palazzo-Craig, Janet.
The battle at Toad Hall.

(Kenneth Grahame's The wind in the willows; 4)
Summary: After escaping from prison disguised as a washerwoman, Toad finds that his house has been taken over by stoats and weasels.
[1. Toads—Fiction] I. Baer, Mary Alice, ill.
II. Grahame, Kenneth, 1859-1932. Wind in the willows.
III. Title. IV. Series: Palazzo-Craig, Janet. Kenneth Grahame's The wind in the willows; 4.
PZ7.P1762Bat [Fic] 81-16407
ISBN 0-89375-642-3 (lib. bdg.) AACR2
ISBN 0-89375-643-1 (pbk.)

Printed in the United States of America
10 9 8 7 6 5 4 3 2 1

Sunlight streamed through the bushes where the Toad lay sleeping. The Toad was dreaming that his toes were icy cold. And, in fact, they were, for he had spent a very cold night sleeping beneath the stars.

He awoke, rubbing his eyes and then his toes. For a moment, he wondered where he was. And then he remembered everything! He remembered that day long ago when he had taken a motor-car. That's when all his troubles began! He had been sent to jail. But dressed as a washerwoman, he'd walked right past the guards and out of the prison. It had been one daring adventure after another, and at last, Toad was free!

Today he would set out for Toad Hall, the home he missed so much. And he would soon see his friends, the Badger, the Mole, and the Rat. Eager to begin the journey home, Toad straightened his washerwoman's skirt and put on his shawl and bonnet.

He marched along a dusty road, and soon he came to a canal. As he stood, wondering which way to go, along came a barge, pulled by an old horse. The barge was steered by a large woman wearing a sun bonnet. "Good morning, ma'am!" she called to the Toad.

“It is indeed a nice morning,” replied the Toad politely, “for those who are not in trouble the way I am. I’ve had to leave my business—I’m in the washing and laundry line, you see. I’m on my way to a place near Toad Hall. But I’ve lost all my money, and I’ve lost my way.”

"Near Toad Hall?" said the woman. "I'm going that way. Hop aboard." As they floated down the canal, the bargewoman said, "So—you're in the washing business?"

"Oh, yes," the Toad answered, "and I love my work, too. I'm never so happy as when I've got both arms in the washtub."

"Well, it's good luck that you're here, then," said the bargewoman.

“What do you mean?” asked the Toad uneasily. For, if the truth were told, the Toad did not have the slightest idea of how to wash clothes.

“There’s a heap of dirty clothes over there,” the woman went on. “While I’m steering, why don’t you do some washing? Then I’ll know you’re enjoying yourself.”

"Oh, no—why don't you let me steer?" said the Toad. "And then you can do the washing in your own way."

"Let you steer?" replied the bargewoman, laughing. "Oh, no. It's dull work, and I want you to be happy."

Grumbling, Toad filled a washtub. He punched and rubbed and slapped at the clothes, but still they sat in a wet heap, as dirty as ever. Then he noticed that his paws were getting all crinkly from being in the water so long. When the soap slipped and flew out of his paws for the fiftieth time, he lost his temper.

Behind him, he heard the bargewoman laughing loudly. "You've never so much as washed a dish cloth in your life, I'll bet."

"How dare you talk to me like that," shouted the Toad. "I'll have you know I am the well-known and highly respected Toad!" At this, the woman came closer and lifted Toad's bonnet.

"Why, so you are," she said. "A horrid, nasty, crawly Toad!" And she picked him up by one leg and tossed him into the canal.

The Toad came up spluttering and swam to shore. Furiously gathering his wet skirts above his knees, he ran to the horse and untied him. He hopped on the horse's back and rode away. The woman was left on the barge, angrily shouting and waving her arms.

Very pleased with himself, the Toad rode into the woods. He had gone quite a long way, when he realized how hungry he was.

As if in answer to these thoughts, a thin stream of smoke reached the Toad's nose. He followed the smoke until he found a campfire. There sat a gypsy, stirring a large pot of stew. Toad sniffed and sniffed the delicious smells of the hot stew. Soon the gypsy looked up and said, "Want to sell that horse of yours?"

After a good bit of bargaining back and forth, the Toad and the gypsy made a deal. Then the Toad sat down to more than one plate of stew. He thought that he had never eaten so good a breakfast in all his life.

Toad marched away in very high spirits. As he walked along, he sang out, "Ho, ho—what a clever Toad I am! There is surely no animal equal to me for cleverness in all the world!"

When Toad reached a big road, he heard the sound of a motor-car. "I'll ask them for a ride," he thought. "Perhaps they will even drive me right up to Toad Hall. Won't Badger and Mole and Rat be surprised!" The car slowed down as it came near him. Suddenly Toad's knees began to shake. He fell to the ground in a faint. "Oh, stupid, stupid Toad," he thought to himself. For as the car came closer, he saw it was the very same one he had taken on that unlucky day long ago.

“How sad—” said one of the men in the car, “a poor washerwoman has fainted in the road. We must help her.” They gently lifted him into the car. When Toad realized that they did not recognize him, he grew a bit braver. He opened one eye and then the other. “Look,” cried one of the gentlemen, “the fresh air is doing her good.”

“Thank you, sir,” said Toad in a feeble voice. And then he grew bolder. “If I may, sir, could I sit in the front seat, where I’ll get the fresh air in my face?”

"What a sensible woman!" said the man. So they helped Toad into the front seat, next to the driver.

Toad felt very brave by this time. Before he could stop himself, he blurted out, "Please, may I drive the car a bit?" The driver laughed very hard and said, "I like your spirit, ma'am! Let's let her have a try—she won't do any harm."

Toad eagerly scrambled into the driver's seat. He drove slowly at first. But then he went a little faster, then faster still. He heard one of the men say, "Be careful, washerwoman!"

"Washerwoman, indeed!" he shouted. "I am the Toad! The motor-car snatcher! The Toad who always escapes!"

“Seize him!” they cried. But before they could, Toad drove the car straight into a muddy pond. Next thing he knew, Toad was flying through the air like a bird. Then with a great splash, he landed in a rushing river.

Struggling and choking, the Toad tried to swim. But the water pulled him quickly along. ‘‘Oh, my,’’ gasped the poor Toad, ‘‘if ever I steal a motor-car again! If ever I sing another boastful song—’’ Then down he went. When he came up, he saw a hole in the river bank ahead. As the water carried him past the hole, he reached out and held onto the edge of it.

He puffed and panted, staring into the hole. And then he saw a face staring back at him. It was his friend the Rat! The Rat put out his paw and pulled Toad in by the neck.

"Oh, Ratty!" Toad cried. "I've been through such times! But it's lucky I'm a smart Toad and made it all turn out all right!"

"Toad," said the Rat firmly, "stop your boasting and take off that *horrible* dress. I'll get you some dry clothes."

After Toad had changed his clothes, he said, "I've so much to tell you and Mole and Badger. We must all go to Toad Hall and celebrate my return."

"Toad Hall?" said the Rat. "You mean you haven't heard?" The Rat told him that Toad Hall had been taken over by the Stoats and Weasels. They'd moved in and told everyone that they had come to stay for good. Badger and Mole were now faithfully camped outside the gates of Toad Hall, keeping an eye on things.

As the Rat finished speaking, there was a knock at the door. The Mole and the Badger entered. "Hurrah!" shouted the Mole, happy to see the Toad. "It's good to have you back!" But the Badger just said,"Welcome, Toad. But alas, it is a sad welcome home—for you have no home!"

The Toad looked worried to hear this. But at that moment, the Rat brought out some lunch, and they all sat down to eat. Afterward, the Rat said, "What shall we do about Toad Hall?"

Mole began, "Here's what I think—" and the Toad said, "No, I'll tell you what we should do—" And soon all three were shouting loudly at one another.

Finally, the Badger said, "Quiet! Here is what we'll do—" The Badger had found out that the Stoats and Weasels were planning a birthday party for the Chief Weasel. Badger also knew of a secret passage in Toad Hall, which led right beneath the dining hall. "In the middle of their party—when they least expect it—we'll surprise them!" Badger said.

All afternoon, the Rat ran around to each of his friends, saying, "Here's a pistol for you and you and you and me. Here's a stick for you and you and you and me. Here's a sword for you and you and you and me."

They waited until the sun went down. Then they made their way to Toad Hall. As they crawled along the secret passage, they heard the Stoats and Weasels above them. "What a time they're having," said the Badger, as they listened to loud laughter and the stamping of feet.

Suddenly, the Badger threw open the trap door, shouting, "Follow me!" What a squealing and squeaking and screeching filled the air! The four brave heroes swung their sticks, whacking and walloping many heads and tails. Shrieking and screaming, the terrified Stoats and Weasels leaped out the doors and windows.

Soon the battle was over. The Badger, in the plain way he had of speaking, said, "I want some grub, I do. Look lively, Toad!" And the four made a very good meal out of the food left behind at the Chief Weasel's birthday party.

The following morning, the Mole, the Rat, and the Badger told the Toad, "You really ought to have a banquet to celebrate your homecoming—it's expected of you." And so the Toad wrote out invitations. But, first, his friends made him promise that he would not boast or brag about his many deeds and misdeeds. He also promised that this time he was through with motor-cars forever.

The guests all cheered as Toad greeted them that night. But true to his word, Toad only smiled humbly and never said a boastful word. There was much feasting and laughter that evening. But, in a way, everyone sort of missed Toad's proud speeches. Things weren't quite so much fun without them. But, try as they might, the guests could get no more than a quiet smile from the Toad. He was, indeed, a very different Toad—at least, until the next time!